Friends
and
Brothers

'You say that word just once more,' said
William to Charlie, 'and I'll hit you.'

Charlie said it.

William hit him.

Charlie let out a screech and kicked
William on the shin, and William bellowed.

William and Charlie's mother came
rushing in like a whirlwind, with a face
like thunder.

'You two will drive me mad!' she
stormed. 'All you do is fight, all day long!'

Vivien Rothwell MacDonald
2006, London,

Also by Dick King-Smith

Lightning Strikes Twice

Friends and Brothers

by Dick King-Smith
pictures by Susan Hellard

mammoth

First published in 1987
by William Heinemann Limited
Reprinted 1988
Paperback edition published 1989 by Mammoth
an imprint of Egmont Children's Books Ltd
Michelin House, 81 Fulham Road, London SW3 6RB

Reprinted 1989 (twice), 1990 (three times), 1991 (twice),
1992 (twice), 1993 (twice), 1994, 1995 (twice), 1996 (twice),
1997, 1998 (twice)

© Text Dick King-Smith 1987
© Illustrations Susan Hellard 1987

ISBN 0 7497 0048 3

A CIP catalogue record for this title
is available from the British Library

Printed and bound in Great Britain
by Cox & Wyman Ltd, Reading, Berkshire

Contents

Friends
and
Brothers

Friends and Brothers

"You say that word just once more," said William to Charlie, "and I'll hit you."

Charlie said it.

William hit him.

Charlie then let out a screech and kicked William on the shin, and William bellowed.

William and Charlie's mother came rushing in like a whirlwind, with a face like thunder.

"You two will drive me mad!" she stormed. "All you do is fight, all day long!"

"William hit me," said Charlie.

"Why did you hit him, William?"

"Because Charlie keeps on saying the same word. Whatever I say, he says the

9

same word, over and over again. Anyway, he kicked me."

"Will hit me first," said Charlie.

"William," said his mother, "you are not to hit Charlie. He is younger than you and much smaller. The next time you do, I shall hit you."

"You didn't ought to, Mum," said William.

"Why not?"

"I'm younger than you and much smaller."

"Absolutely," said Charlie.

"There you are!" shouted William madly. "That's the word! Whatever I say, he just says 'Absolutely'. He doesn't even know what it means."

"Absolutely," said Charlie.

William let out a yell of rage and rushed at his brother with his fists clenched. Charlie dodged behind his mother, who held the furious William at arm's length.

"Now *stop* it, the pair of you!" she said. "William, you stop attacking Charlie, and Charlie, you stop annoying Will. I cannot

stand one more minute of being shut in this house with you two. Get your bikes. We'll go to the Park."

William stumped off, limping slightly from the kick, and shouting angrily "It's not fair!"

From behind his mother's back, Charlie's face appeared. Silently he mouthed the word 'Absolutely'.

In the park, William rode his BMX at top speed. He felt the need to be all by himself, miles from anybody. The roads in the Park were full of steep switchback slopes, and William swooped down them flat out. Like a lot of elder brothers, he felt he had had a raw deal.

Charlie, meanwhile, was trying to see
how slowly he could pedal without falling
off. He had not long inherited William's old
bike and was fascinated by the problems of
balance. This was much more fun than a
tricycle. Like a lot of younger brothers, he
had forgotten all about the recent row, and
was singing happily to himself. Then he
came to the top of one of the steepest slopes.
He grinned, and bent low over the
handlebars.

His mother, walking some way behind, saw the small figure disappear from view. A moment later, a dreadful wailing started her running hard.

Halfway down the slope, Charlie lay sprawled in the road, the old bike beside him, one wheel still spinning. His face, she saw when she reached him, was covered in blood. There was a deep cut across his forehead and a set of long scratches, gravel-studded, down one cheek.

At that moment William came flying back down the reverse slope and skidded to a halt, wide-eyed with horror at the scene.

"What happened?" he said miserably.

"I don't know. He must have touched the brakes and gone straight over the handlebars. Listen carefully, Will. We must get him to hospital quickly – that cut's going to need stitches. I'm going to carry him to the nearest Park gate, that one over there, and try and stop a car to give us a lift. Can you wheel both bikes and stick them out of sight in those bushes, and then run and catch me up?"

"Yes, Mum," said William.

He looked at his brother's face. Charlie was still crying, but quietly now.

"He'll be all right, won't he?" William said.

Twenty-four hours later Charlie, recovered now from the shock of his accident, was jabbering away nineteen to the dozen.

He remembered little of the actual crash, or of his treatment in hospital, the stitching of the cut and the cleaning-up of his gravelly face. It was very swollen now, so that one side of him didn't look like Charlie at all, but his voice was as loud and piercing as ever as he plied his brother with endless questions.

"Did you see me come off, Will?"

"No."

"I went right over the handlebars, didn't I?"

"Suppose so."

"How fast d'you think I was going, Will?"

"I don't know."

"A hundred miles an hour, d'you think?" squeaked Charlie excitedly.

"I expect so, Charles," said William in a kindly voice. "You looked an awful mess when I got there."

"Lots of blood, Will?"

"Yes. Ugh, it was horrible."

"Then what happened?"

"Well, Mum ran all the way to the nearest gate carrying you, and a kind lady in a car stopped and gave us all a lift to the hospital."

"And then they stitched me up!" said Charlie proudly.

"Yes."

"Did you see them stitching me up, Will?"

"No, Charles."

"I expect it was a huge great needle," said Charlie happily. "You've never had six stitches, have you, Will?"

"No," said William. "You were jolly brave, Charlie," he said. "You can have a go on my BMX when you're better."

"I can't reach the pedals," Charlie said.

"Oh. Well, you can take a picture with my Instamatic if you like."

"Can I really, Will?"

"And you can borrow my Swiss Army knife for a bit."

"Can I really?"

"Yes," said William. He put his hand in his pocket and pulled out a rather squidgy-looking bar of chocolate.

"And you can have half of this," he said.

"Gosh, thanks, Will!"

William and Charlie's mother put her head round the door, wondering at the unaccustomed silence, and saw her sons sitting side by side on Charlie's bed, chewing chocolate. William actually had his arm round Charlie's shoulders.

"Look what I've got, Mum," said Charlie with his mouth full.

"Did you give him some of yours, Will?" said his mother.

"Naturally," said William loftily. "We're friends and brothers."

Another day went by, and Charlie was definitely better. His face was much less swollen, his spirits high, his voice shriller yet.

He had made up a song about his exploits, which he sang, endlessly and very loudly.

"Who came rushing down the hill?
Charlie boy!
Who had such an awful spill?
Charlie boy!
Who came down with a terrible thud,
Covered in mud and covered in blood?
Charlie, Charlie, Charlie boy!"

William, as he occasionally did, had an attack of earache, painful enough without Charlie's singing.

"Charles," he said as the friend and brother was just about to come rushing down the hill for the twentieth time, "d'you think you could keep a bit quiet?"

"Why?" shouted Charlie at the top of his voice.

"Because I've got earache."

"Oh," said Charlie in a whisper. "Oh, sorry, Will. Does it hurt a lot?"

"Yes," said William, white-faced, "it does."

For the rest of the day Charlie tiptoed about the house, occasionally asking William if he needed anything, and, if he did, fetching it. He guarded his brother's peace and quiet fiercely, frowning angrily at his mother when she dropped a saucepan on the kitchen floor.

"Hullo, Charlie boy!" shouted his father on his return from work. "How's the poor old face?"

"Don't make such a noise, Dad!" hissed Charlie furiously. "Will's got earache."

It was now a week since Charlie's accident, a week of harmony and brotherly love.

Charlie's face was now miles better and William's earache quite gone.

They were drawing pictures, at the kitchen table, with felt pens.

"Charles," said William. "Can I borrow your red? Mine's run out."

"No," said Charlie.

"Why not? You're not using it."

"Yes, I am," said Charlie, picking up his red felt and colouring with it.

"You just did that to be annoying," said William angrily.

The word 'annoying' rang a bell with Charlie, and he grinned and nodded and said "Absolutely!"

"Charlie!" said William between his teeth. "Don't start that again or I'll hit you!"

"You can't," said Charlie. "I've got a bad face."

"I'll hit you all the same," said William.

"I'll shout in your bad ear," said Charlie, "and d'you know what I'll shout?"

"What?"

"ABSOLUTELY!!" yelled Charlie and scuttled out of the room with William in hot pursuit, as life returned to normal.

On the Other Hand

"Will," said Charlie. "What's the opposite of right?"

"What?" said William, who was busy reading.

"It's a really hard one this, Will. What's the opposite of right?"

"Left," said William.

"Wrong," said Charlie.

William put his book down.

"Don't be stupid, Charles," he said. He spread his arms wide, hands open, fingers outstretched.

"Look," he said. "This one's right, this one's left. Opposites. See?"

"But that's not the right answer," said

Charlie patiently. "I told you it was a hard one. The right answer's 'wrong'."

William felt his patience slipping.

"How can the right answer be wrong?" he said.

"Because 'wrong' is the opposite of 'right'," said Charlie.

"So is 'left'."

"Oh, I know that," said Charlie airily, "but that's the easy answer."

"Mum," said William.

"Yes?"

"What's the opposite of 'right'?"

"Well, it depends, Will. It could be 'left' or it could be 'wrong'."

"You knew," said William glumly.

Charlie meanwhile was quizzing his father, who was writing a letter.

"Dad," said Charlie.

"Yes?"

"What's the opposite of right?"

Charlie's father put down his pen and turned to face his younger son.

"Well, Charlie," he said, "there are several possible answers to that question. First of all, if you were talking about your hands or your feet or your eyes, you could say the opposite of 'right' was 'left'."

"Or your ears," said Charlie.

"What? Oh yes, or your ears. But, on the other hand, if you were doing a sum, adding 5 to 5, let's say, then the answer 10 would be right and the answer 9 would be wrong."

"Or 8," Charlie said.

"What? Oh yes, or 8. But then again, Charlie, there's a third answer to your question, you see."

"There is?" said Charlie.

"Yes. Now – what am I doing?"

"Talking a lot."

"No, I mean what was I doing when you started asking me?"

"Writing a letter."

26

"Exactly. Now, here's a third answer to your question. Ask it again."

"What's the opposite of right, Dad?"

"Don't write."

"Eh?"

"Yes, Charlie," said his father. He took out a fresh sheet of paper and picked up his pen.

"Now," he said, "you say to me – 'Write!'"

"Right," said Charlie.

Obediently, his father scribbled away.

"Now," he said, "say the opposite."

"Wrong," said Charlie.

His father went on writing.

"Left," said Charlie.

His father still went on writing.

"Oh, now I get it!" said Charlie, "Don't write!" and immediately the flying pen skidded to a halt. Charlie considered this. Then he said "Can I have that piece of paper, Dad?"

He went away and found himself a felt pen and wrote on the paper in big red letters

RITE   LEFD
RITE   RONG
RITE   DOAN TRITE

Then he went to find his brother. He showed him the paper.

"Look, Will," he said, "there's *three* opposites. Dad showed me. There's another sort, when you're writing a letter."

William read what Charlie had written.

"Charles!" he said scornfully. "You've

spelt every word wrong. You're hopeless at spelling, hopeless. You can't even spell little short words like these."

"I'm only good at really long words," said Charlie. "I could beat you at spelling a really long word."

"Don't be so stupid."

Charlie went away, his eyes narrowed in thought. He went to his bedroom and chose an animal book from his bookshelf and took it to the bathroom and locked himself in. He turned the pages till he found the picture of a particular animal, and propped the open book on top of the lavatory cistern. Then, sitting the wrong way round on the lavatory seat cover, he copied carefully in small letters onto the small palm of his left hand:

RHI
NOC
ERO
S

At supper time Charlie said to his father "Dad, why's a rhinoceros called a rhinoceros?"

"Well," said his father, "the name comes from two old Greek words, 'rhinos', which means 'nose', and 'keras', which means 'horn'. 'Nose – horn', you see? An animal with a horn on its nose."

"It's a long word, isn't it, Dad?" said Charlie.

William rose to the bait.

"Charlie says he's only good at spelling long words!" he said.

"I am," said Charlie.

"Well, go on then," said William. "Spell rhinoceros."

"Oh, come on, Will!" said his mother. "That's much too hard for Charlie. I don't suppose you could spell it yourself."

"I bet I could."

"Go on then."

"All right," said William. "R – I – . . . " he began and his mother and father laughed.

"You're wrong already," they said.

"Can I try?" said Charlie in a small polite voice.

Now it was William's turn to laugh.

"Fat chance you've got of getting it right if I can't," he scoffed.

"I might," Charlie said.

"Have a go," said his father.

"Yes, go on, Charlie, have a try," said his mother.

Charlie rested his right elbow on the table and with his right hand scratched his head and frowned as though he was thinking very hard. His left hand was curved around his plate, the palm towards him.

Slowly, pausing here and there as though for an extra effort of thought, he said "R...H...I...N.....O.......C..E....R......O..S."

"Hurray!" cried his mother.

"Clever old Charlie!" shouted his father.

William's mouth hung open in amazement.

"Did he get it right?" he said.

"Yes!" they said. "He did!"

"Yes," said Charlie. "I'm good at spelling long words, Will, I told you. I was right. And you were the opposite. You do know what the opposite of 'right' is, don't you, Will?"

Snapdragon

Charlie had a pet beetle. It was quite an ordinary-looking beetle, except for its colour, which was a shiny dark red.

Charlie, who was keen on gardening and knew the names of a lot of flowers, had found it climbing up an antirrhinum, so of course he called it Snapdragon.

Snapdragon did not live up to his fierce name. He did not bite or sting, and he allowed Charlie to take him to school (in a matchbox) and show him off. Even Charlie's teacher did not know what kind of beetle Snapdragon was, which – combined with his colour – made him seem all the rarer and more remarkable.

"He might be the only one," said Charlie to William.

"The only one what?"

"The only one of his kind of beetle."

"Don't be silly, Charles," said William loftily. "He must have had a mother and a father just the same as him."

"He might have come out of an egg," Charlie said.

"Well, eggs have mothers and fathers, don't they?"

"He might have been an orphan egg," said Charlie, turning away.

"Oh, don't be so stupid, Charlie," said William angrily, "and I wish you'd shut up about your beastly beetle. I'm sick and tired of him."

William made a horrible face behind his brother's back, changing it quickly into a mad grin as Charlie turned round again.

"And I should think everyone else is fed up with him too," he said.

"I'm not," said Charlie, putting Snapdragon in his matchbox and sliding it shut. "I think he's lovely."

"Well, no one else does."

"Yes they do. Mandy and Laura do."

Mandy and Laura were in Charlie's class and he particularly liked them. Usually William did not tease his brother about this, but when he did feel like getting Charlie's goat there was one sure way to do it.

"Oh, Mandy and Laura!" he said scornfully. "Your girl-friends!"

These words, William knew, drove Charlie into a wild rage, and now he rushed at William in such fury that he dropped the matchbox on the floor.

Much later, when William and Charlie's mother had broken up the fight, William came back into the room and saw the box lying there. He picked it up and opened it. Inside, Snapdragon was quite still.

Is he dead, William wondered, and he gave the beetle a little prod with his finger.

Immediately, Snapdragon opened a pair of small curved wings and flew out of the

36

matchbox and out of the open window and away.

William thought quickly. No good leaving the box wide open – it would be plain that he had done it. No use shutting it right up – how then could Snapdragon have escaped? Carefully he closed it so as to leave a small gap at one end, a gap just big enough for a beetle to have crawled through, and put it down on the floor again. Then he slipped quietly out of the house and went to play with his friends Sam and Weasel.

Luckily it was William and Charlie's mother who picked up the matchbox and opened it and found it empty. Luckily she came to the conclusion that William had hoped for.

"What must have happened, you see," she said to Charlie, "was that when you dropped it, it slid open just enough for Snapdragon to get out. He's sure to be somewhere in the room. I'll help you look."

But though they searched everywhere, there was no sign of the escaped prisoner, and Charlie was very unhappy.

"I'll tell you what," said his mother. "When I make a cake for your birthday next week, I'll make a chocolate Snapdragon, a big one, to go on the top."

In the days that followed, William began to feel more and more guilty about Snapdragon. It would have been better, he felt, if someone had actually accused him but no one had. He thought about confessing but decided against it. Instead he had a sudden brilliant idea.

There was a shop that he knew where they sold all kinds of small toy ornaments, mostly little models of animals in wood or pottery or glass. Some were made out of sea-shells stuck together, and one of these was actually a beetle. It had a big oval shell for a body and a small round one for a head and little twisty pointed shells for legs. It was even a reddish colour. It was also

39

rather expensive but William was determined to buy it for a birthday present for his brother. Then he wouldn't need to feel guilty any more. He unscrewed the plate in the belly of his piggy-bank.

As well as William and Charlie, there were seven other children at the birthday party.

"Who d'you want to invite, Charlie?" his mother had said.

"Mandy and Laura and Ruth and Justine," said Charlie. He stared beadily at William, waiting for him to say "All your girl-friends!" and ready to attack him the moment he said it, but William kept silent.

Charlie was so surprised at this that he began to feel a little guilty.

"You can ask someone if you like, Will," he said.

"Can I have Sam and Weasel?" William said. Weasel was Sam's little brother. His real name was Oliver, but no one ever called him that.

"And how about Hannah, Will?" said his mother. "She is your girl-friend."

"She's not!" shouted Charlie angrily. "She's his friend!" and he stamped out of the room. William grinned happily.

When Charlie opened his presents on the morning of his birthday, there was nothing from William.

"Haven't you got a present for Charlie?" his parents said.

"Yes," said William. "It's a surprise."

"Well, aren't you going to give it to him?"

"Later," William said.

The children sat round the table staring at the big oblong chocolate cake and especially at the thing that stood on top of it.

"It's a beautiful beetle," said Hannah.

"It's really lifelike," said Sam.

"It's just like Snapdragon," said Mandy and Laura together.

"Only miles bigger," said Ruth.

"At least twenty times as big," said Justine.

"Can I have a bit?" said Weasel.

William said nothing. His hand was in his pocket, holding something.

"Come on, Charlie," said his mother. "You've got to cut the cake, and then we'll sing 'Happy Birthday'. But I think I'd better take Snapdragon off first, hadn't I?"

"No!" shouted Charlie. "I want to have him!" and he grabbed at the chocolate beetle so roughly that its head broke away and its legs snapped off and its body cracked into pieces.

Charlie broke into terrible sobs. He wept bitterly, his head bowed over the broken bits of beetle on his plate.

"Don't cry, Charlie!" said Hannah and Mandy and Laura and Ruth and Justine, and those nearest to him patted him in a motherly way.

"It's only chocolate, Charlie," said Sam. "You can still eat it just the same."

"Can I have a bit now?" said Weasel.

While they were all busy comforting Charlie, William took the sea-shell beetle out of his pocket and stood it carefully on top of the cake. He waited till Charlie's sobs had become snuffles, and then he said in a loud voice "Happy birthday, Charles".

"Oh!" cried all the girls. "Look, Charlie! Look what Will's given you! Isn't it lovely?"

"Oh, Will," said his mother, "that really is beautiful. Look, Charlie! What do you say?"

Still sniffing, Charlie looked up. There were tears on his cheeks and his nose was running, and Mandy and Laura, sitting either side, mopped him with paper napkins. Then Charlie reached out, slowly this time, and lifted the sea-shell beetle off the cake. He looked at it and managed a sort of smile.

"Thanks, Will," he said. "It's nice."

"Come on," his mother said. "Let's cut the cake. I'll help you. Sing, everybody."

And they all sang "Happy Birthday, dear Charlie, Happy Birthday to you," and so it was.

Not Enough Cornflakes

It was the day of the Marathon.

The race was to begin in the Park, not half a mile from William and Charlie's house, and the boys were going to be taken to watch the start.

William was daydreaming over his cornflakes.

He saw in his mind, not the start, but the finish of the Marathon. Huge excited crowds lined the streets, cheering madly, one name on everyone's lips. "William! William!" they shouted. "William's in the lead, William's going to win!" and every eye was fixed on the bend where the runners would come into view as they entered

45

the finishing straight.

First, two policemen on motor-bikes roared round the corner, followed by a police car with its headlights blazing and its siren blaring *Nee—nah! Nee—nah! Nee—nah!*

Then at last appeared the figure of a runner – quite alone, for he had long outdistanced all the other thousands of competitors.

The figure was wearing . . . (William took

an absent-minded mouthful of cornflakes as he thought about this) . . . was wearing . . . green shorts and . . . blue-and-white trainers and . . . a yellow T-shirt . . . with black lettering on it. What did the lettering say? William chewed and swallowed and suddenly he began to smile broadly.

WILL POWER

that's what the lettering said!

And now he was nearing the finishing line, while all around the crowd went wild. He could hear them, as he broke the tape, all yelling the same thing. "William the Conqueror!" they shouted. "William the Conqueror!"

But then gradually the hundreds of voices became one voice, and that voice was a familiar squeaky one.

"William, you're bonkers!" Charlie was saying, peering round the cornflake packet.

"William's bonkers!" he said to his parents. "I've been watching him, and first he was puffing and panting as if he'd been running and then he started grinning all over his face and then just now he raised both arms in the air! William, you're bonkers!"

William glowered.

"I was thinking," he said.

"Well, think about eating up your breakfast," said his mother, "or we'll be late for the start of the Marathon. You too, Charlie — stop reading that cornflake packet and get a move on."

Charlie, though as yet not the world's best speller, was a good reader. While his brother had been dreaming, he had been hatching a plan of action, and what he was reading on the back of the cornflake packet interested him greatly. It said:

For Energy   – Enriched Wheat Flakes
For Stamina – Sugar
For Strength – Iron
For Vigour   – Vitamins C, B6, and D

Eagerly, Charlie began to eat.

"I don't know what's up with Charlie today," said his mother as they made their way across the Park, Charlie running ahead, William dawdling behind. "You were reading your newspaper so you didn't see, but he ate four helpings of cornflakes in the time it took William to finish one."

"Doesn't seem to have done him much harm," said Charlie's father. "Just look at him."

Before them was a throng of people making their way towards the start of the

Marathon, and Charlie scampered madly about amongst them at top speed. He was wearing a red-and-yellow-striped cap with a long peak, and he buzzed in and out of the forest of legs like a bee in a flower-bed. Catching sight of his family, he came zooming back.

"You're full of energy today," said his father.

"And stamina!" shouted Charlie. "And strength! And vigour! Come on, Will, I'll race you!"

"Oh, get lost, Charlie!" said William.

"That's just what he will get," said his mother, "if he doesn't stay close to us."

At the start line of the Marathon there were thousands of runners, men and women, youngish and middle-aged and some quite old. Most wore singlets and running shorts, but there were lots of strange outfits too.

Some were dressed as waiters, carrying trays of drinks, some were dressed in animal costumes – a monkey, a bear, a frog. There were two people inside a pantomime horse, and one spectacular entry – nine men forming a long green caterpillar.

The watching crowd was so huge that it was not possible to get anywhere near the actual start; and when at last the starting-pistol cracked and the ground shook as the army of runners set off on their 26-miles-and-385 yards journey, William and Charlie's father hoisted William onto his shoulders so that he could see over the heads of the spectators. And William and Charlie's mother bent down to pick up Charlie. But

Charlie had gone.

"Charlie's gone!" she shouted above the noise of the crowd.

"Oh, Lor! Where on earth's he got to?"

Forgetting the runners now streaming past them, they were looking frantically around when suddenly, from his high perch, William cried "Look! There he is!"

They looked, as the really good runners went racing away across the Park, and they saw the not-so-good runners plodding past, and the not-very-good-at-all runners

approaching. These were followed by some
waiters balancing their trays, and then by
the monkey, the bear, and the frog, which
was hopping. Behind them trotted the pantomime horse, and behind the horse the
nine-man caterpillar rippled along.

But last of all, scuttling along as fast as he
could go, came a very small figure wearing a
red-and-yellow-striped cap with a long
peak.

"Charlie!" yelled William in wild excitement as the smallest Marathon runner went

by, hard on the last pair of heels of the caterpillar. "Charlie! Good old Charlie!" and the people around took up his cry.

"Good old Charlie!" – the roar went all down the ranks of the crowd, until at last the family caught up with the runaway, who had stopped, puffed.

"Gosh, Charlie!" panted William, for once frankly admiring, "You ran in the Marathon!"

"I did, didn't I?" squeaked Charlie excitedly. "How far d'you think I ran, Mum?"

His mother looked back across the Park to the start-line.

"About 385 yards, I should think," she said.

"How much further have I got to go, Dad?"

"26 miles."

"Oh," said Charlie.

"You wouldn't get there till about to-morrow night, Charles," said William.

"Oh," said Charlie.

He looked into the distance, where now

54

there were no runners to be seen. Even the caterpillar had disappeared.

"Let's go home," said his mother.

"It's tiring, running the Marathon, I should think," said his father.

"That was the trouble," said Charlie thoughtfully. "I didn't have enough cornflakes."

Happy Birthday

It was William's birthday. One of the family's customs was that, on your birthday, you could choose your own special breakfast.

William had chosen poached eggs. He was sitting at the table waiting for them, wearing the best of all his birthday presents. This was a chimpanzee mask, not just an ordinary flat mask with two eye-holes and a nose-hole, but a very superior one.

It was moulded in the exact shape of a chimpanzee's jutting face, and best of all, the lower jaw was hinged. When you opened your own mouth, a strap that fitted under your chin made the mouth of the mask open too.

To top it all, there was a shaggy wig of coarse black hair

To William's father coming into the room, the whole effect was horribly lifelike.

"Ugh!" he said. "You look frightful, Will! What have you chosen for your birthday breakfast?"

"Hoo! Hoo!" said William, parting his jaws to expose two rows of large yellow teeth.

"That's Chimpanzee for poached eggs," said Charlie. "Isn't it, Will?"

"Hoo!" said William.

He scratched his ribs and grunted with excitement, bouncing up and down in his chair.

"Why are they called 'poached' eggs, Mum?" said Charlie.

"Well, you use this special kind of pan," said his mother, "where the eggs sit in these little metal nests and are cooked slowly by the steam from the boiling water underneath. That's called poaching. This pan is a poacher. And these eggs are ready. Take off your mask, Will – you can't eat with that thing on."

"Oh, Mum!" protested the chimpanzee.

"William!"

"Oh, all right."

But when breakfast was over, William went ape again. He was expecting his friend Sam, and he set Charlie on guard at the window.

After a while, Charlie said "He's coming, Will! Sam's coming down the road. And

Weasel too."

"Hoo, hoo, hoo!" said William softly, and he hid in the hall.

When the bell rang, Charlie opened the front door.

"Hullo," said Sam, but before he could say anything else a frightful creature leaped out of the shadows, shaking its hairy locks and snapping its fearful jaws and screaming the awful tearing screams of an angry chimpanzee.

Sam took one look and burst out laughing.

Weasel took one look and burst into tears.

Once Weasel had been comforted and he and Sam had been shown William's other presents, they all decided to go and play hide-and-seek in the wood at the bottom of the garden.

"I'll be first to hide," said the chimpanzee, "because it's my birthday. Count to 100 before you come looking," and he shambled away with bent knees and arms swinging from side to side so low that his knuckles almost brushed the ground. Once out of sight of the others, he found beside the path a leafy tree with low spreading branches and climbed into it and settled down to wait.

When the seekers had reached 100, they set out together. It was a dull day and the wood was rather dark and silent and Weasel reached for Sam's hand. They followed the path on which they had seen William set out, until, as they walked under a leafy tree with low spreading branches, Sam suddenly hissed "Look out! Take cover! Get behind this tree!"

"What is it?" whispered Charlie as the three of them crouched behind the trunk of the tree.

"It's a poacher!" said Sam.

"What's a poacher?" asked Weasel in a shaky voice.

Charlie patted him.

"It's all right, Weasel," he said. "It's only a special kind of pan for cooking eggs in."

"Ssssh!" said Sam. "He's coming this

way. He's got a gun."

Weasel whimpered.

Down the path towards them came a big boy carrying an air-rifle. When he reached the tree and saw the seekers crouching there, he pointed the air-rifle towards them and said in a nasty voice "Push off, you kids."

Weasel began to cry.

"It's not your wood," Sam said.

"And you shouldn't point guns," Charlie said.

"I'll do more than point it if you don't push off," said the big boy. "I'll . . . " but before he could say any more there was a rustling sound overhead, and as he looked up, a frightful face peered out of the leaves above him and shook its hairy locks and snapped its fearful jaws and screamed the awful tearing screams of an angry chimpanzee.

With a shout of horror the big boy took to his heels and ran.

Easily, as apes do, the chimpanzee swung down from the branch above and dropped beside them.

"That was fantastic, William!" said Sam, grinning with delight.

"You were brilliant, Will!" shouted Charlie, dancing with excitement.

"I want to go home," snuffled Weasel.

But William did not yet feel ready to speak in his own language. With his

brother and his friends he shambled homewards with bent knees and arms swinging from side to side so low that his knuckles almost brushed the ground. Every now and then he opened his great jaws to utter soft ape-sounds of pure pleasure.

"Hoo, hoo!" said William on his happy birthday. "Hoo, hoo, hoo!"

Cry Wolf

William and Charlie were on holiday with their parents, at an old cottage in the middle of nowhere. It was called Cock Robin Cottage, and all around it was a beautiful landscape of rocky hills and dales, down which flowed clear cold streams.

Every day the family went out in the country and walked up the hills and down the dales and played by the streams. They met few people, but a great many sheep and cattle.

By the end of each day everyone's legs were weary, and the boys were (for once) glad to get into bed and have a story. Both

65

William and Charlie were good readers, but there's something very nice about being read to, when you're tired out. It doesn't have to be a brand-new story; it can be one that you've heard loads of times; and a book that was a great favourite was *Aesop's Fables*.

William preferred the more thoughtful tales, like 'The Dog and the Shadow' or 'The Ass eating Thistles'. But Charlie liked his fables meaty, with plenty of beatings and bloodshed, 'The Horse and the Lion' for example, or 'The Kite, the Frog and the Mouse'.

They took turns to choose.

"Your turn, Charlie," said his mother one evening. "Which one d'you want?"

" 'The Ox and the Frog'," said Charlie. "Where the old frog explodes – Wham! – Powee! – Splat! – bits of frog flying all over the place!"

"We had that," said William, "a couple of nights ago."

"Choose another one, Charlie," said his mother.

66

Charlie cast about in his mind for a bloodthirsty story.

"I know!" he said. " 'The Shepherd's Boy'!"

So their mother read them the story of the boy who looked after some sheep on a common, and, just by way of a joke, kept running to men in nearby fields, yelling "A wolf! A wolf!" And when at last they got fed up with leaving their work to help, only to find the boy was fooling, the wolf did come. And the boy cried "A wolf! A wolf!" in earnest. And no one took a blind bit of notice.

Charlie looked with pleasure at the picture in the book which showed a huge black wolf chewing lumps out of a little white sheep.

"Served the stupid boy right," he said, and he sat up in bed and pointed his nose at the sky and made wolf-howl noises.

"What about the poor old sheep?" said William. "You ought to feel sorry for it."

He thought of all the hundreds of sheep they'd seen that day. He looked out of the

bedroom window and imagined them all lying in the darkness on the lonely hills.

"There couldn't be any wolves about nowadays, could there, Mum?" he said.

"No," said his mother. "The last British one was killed about two hundred years ago, I think."

She said good-night and turned out the light.

William was just getting sleepy when he saw his brother get out of bed and tiptoe to the window and peer out. Then suddenly Charlie scuttled back and leaped onto William's bed and grabbed him in mock terror, shouting "A wolf! A wolf! There's a wolf outside, Will!" and William thumped him and Charlie kicked William and their father came upstairs and was very angry.

Next day, as they set out from Cock Robin Cottage for a walk, William was busy working out a way to pay Charlie back. He was trying to think of other kinds of wild animals with which to frighten his brother.

They walked beside a river, and William thought of crying out "A crocodile! A crocodile!" but that didn't seem likely.

They walked through a patch of very tall grass, just the place where a man-eater might lie in wait, but shouting "A lion! A lion!" or "A tiger! A tiger!" wouldn't, he guessed, be much good either.

He needed to think of a more probable animal that was also big enough and fierce enough.

They came to a thick dark wood and walked in among the trees.

William thought about forests of old and what sort of creatures you might have found in them. Wolves, yes – but they were out. Deer – not scary enough. Wild boar? He tried saying "A wild boar! A wild boar!" quietly to himself, but it didn't sound right.

Bears, thought William suddenly – that's it, bears! I'm sure there were bears in England once. There might be one or two left.

He dropped behind the others, and when they were some way ahead, he suddenly gave a scream and ran towards them with an expression of horror on his face.

"A bear! A bear!" shouted William wildly.

To his disgust, they all laughed.

"Is it the Teddy-Bears' Picnic?" said his father.

"Is it Winnie-the-Pooh?" said his mother.

"Has it got a bear bottom?" said Charlie.

William laughed too. There wasn't much else to do.

I'll think of something, he said to himself. There must be something you could meet on a country walk that people are frightened of, and just at that moment, they came out of the wood and there in front of them was a herd of cows.

Of course, thought William – a bull! Beware of the Bull! Everybody's frightened of bulls, or they jolly well should be. That'll

scare the pants off Charlie!

Once again he hung back, and when they were far enough away, he suddenly gave a scream and ran towards them with an expression of horror on his face.

"A bull! A bull!" shouted William wildly.

This time, because it was a more likely animal, they did actually look round at the peacefully grazing cows, but then they walked on again.

"Give it a rest, William," said his father. "Joke's over."

"Yes, do shut up, Will," said his mother. "You're spoiling the peace and quiet with all that shouting."

As for Charlie, he simply said "Stupid boy!" which annoyed William so much that he thumped him. Then of course William's parents got angry with him, and so once again he walked alone behind the others, scowling and muttering to himself.

Two or three fields further on, there was another herd of cows. By the time William reached the middle of this field, a good hundred yards behind now, the grazing cows were quite close to him, and one of them in particular – a big red one with a white face – raised its head and stared at him as he scuffed his moody way past. Then it blew through its nose.

William glanced up and suddenly he saw that on the end of that nose there was a ring.

As they neared the far end of the field, the others heard a scream and saw William running towards them with an expression of horror on his face, waving his arms and shouting wildly "A bull! A bull!"

This time he did not stop when he reached them, but dashed past at top speed, making for the nearest gate. Endlessly he yelled "A bull! A bull!" and

before any of the others could say anything, they heard a loud snort behind them and saw a large red animal trotting purposefully towards them, swinging its heavy white head in a most unfriendly manner.

"Phew!" gasped William and Charlie's father as they all lay puffing and panting in

the grass on the far safe side of the gate. "I haven't run so fast for years!"

William grinned.

"Well," he said, "You can't say I didn't warn you."

Try Counting Sheep

William and Charlie's mother closed the book.

"Right," she said, "that was a long story. Now, into bed, both of you, and straight to sleep."

William settled himself in the bottom bunk and watched Charlie's skinny little legs climbing the ladder to the top one.

"Mum!" he said in a moany voice.

"What is it, Will?"

"How *can* I go straight to sleep? As soon as you're out of the room, Charlie'll start talking. He talks for hours."

"Well, don't answer him."

"I have to. He's always asking me

79

questions."

"It's because my brain is so busy," said Charlie from the top bunk. "I can't get to sleep because I'm busy thinking things."

"Try counting sheep, Charlie," said his mother. "Just imagine a flock of sheep in a field, and one of them finds a hole in the hedge and hops through it. And then another one follows. And another. And another."

"That's four sheep," said Charlie.

"You don't stop there, Charles," said William scornfully. "You go on counting till all the sheep have got through the hedge."

"Well, how many sheep are there in the field?" asked Charlie.

"As many as it takes to send you to sleep," said his mother. "Good-night now. Sleep tight, mind the fleas don't bite."

Charlie waited till the sound of her footsteps going downstairs had died away, and then he said "Will?"

"What?"

"Why do I have to count sheep? Sheep

81

are boring. I could count fleas, couldn't I?"

"Oh, count anything you like. Just shut up, that's all."

"Instead of sheep hopping through a hedge I could count fleas hopping down from my bunk into yours. Couldn't I?"

William began to scratch.

"You haven't got fleas, have you?" he said.

"No," said Charlie, "but I haven't got sheep either."

"Don't be silly, Charlie," said William. "You don't have to *have* the things you're counting. You just imagine them. You can count anything you like."

"So I could count fleas?"

William scratched again.

"No, not fleas," he said.

"But you just said . . ."

"Oh, do shut up, Charlie. I want to go to sleep. Just think of some other kind of animal and count them."

"What kind?"

William sighed. I'd better suggest something, he thought, or he's never even going to start counting. He suddenly remembered a programme on the telly about African animals, great herds of them stretching for miles and miles, plodding along, one behind the other, never-ending.

"Try counting wildebeests," he said.

"Whatty beasts?"

"Wil. . .de. . .beests," said William.

"What's a Will D. Beast, Will?"

"Well, they're sort of like a horse, the body is, but they've got heads more like a cow. With horns. And a beard."

"The daddy ones have beards, do they?" said Charlie.

"The mummies have beards too."

"Mummies can't have beards. Mummy hasn't got a beard."

"Well, she isn't a wildebeest, is she?"

"If she was," said Charlie, "we'd be little Will D. Beasts. At least you would, Will. You'd be a Will D. Beast."

"Why, what would you be?"

"I'd be a Charlie D. Beast."

"Oh, just stop being so silly, Charles," said William angrily, "and try counting

wildebeests. I want to go to sleep. I'm tired."

For a few minutes there was silence. Then Charlie's face appeared, upside down, as he hung over the edge of his bunk.

"Will?" he said.

"What now?"

"How can I count Will D. Beasts if I

don't know what they look like?" William, who had been lying on his back, suddenly turned on his tummy and began to punch his pillow furiously with both fists. Then he got out of bed and switched on the light. He took an animal book from the bookshelf, found a picture of a wildebeest, and showed it, in silence, to his younger brother.

"Oh, that!" said Charlie. "That's a gnu."

"They're the same animal," William said. He closed the book, put it back on the shelf, turned out the light, and got into bed again.

He said in a careful patient voice "Just try counting them, Charles. Just imagine you're in Africa, watching a huge herd of wildebeests walking past, thousands and thousands and thousands of them. You're sitting there counting them and the sun's blazing down and you're getting very, very sleepy."

At last, above his head, William heard Charlie beginning to count, quite slowly, quite quietly.

"One. . .two. . .three. . ." he began.

He had reached 'twenty' and William's eyelids were just beginning to droop when suddenly Charlie said, loudly and very fast indeed, "twentyonetwentytwotwentythree-twentyfourtwentyfive twentysix twenty-seventwentyeighttwentyninetwentyten. . ."

"Charlie!" cried William. "What are you doing?"

"Not my fault," said Charlie. "The Will D. Beasts were walking quite slowly and

86

then they suddenly started to gallop. There
must have been a lion about.''

Again there was silence for a while, and
then Charlie's duvet came whizzing down
past William's head.

"Charlie!" he said.

"It's terribly hot in Africa," Charlie said.
"I'm thirsty. I'm going to get a drink."

He came down the ladder from the top bunk
and went out to the bathroom. When he had
climbed back into bed again, he said "Will?"

"Now what?"

"What comes after ninety-nine?"

"A hundred, stupid."

"And then two hundred?"

"No, of course not. You have to start again – a hundred and one, a hundred and two," said William.

He pulled his duvet over his face and tried not to hear the steady murmur overhead as the count went on. Once more he had almost drifted off when Charlie said "Will?"

William did not answer. If I keep quiet, he thought, perhaps he will shut up.

"Will, what comes after a million?"

William sat up.

"You can't have counted to a million," he said.

"I haven't. Not yet. I was just wondering."

"Charlie," said William between his teeth. "Go. . .to. . .sleep!"

"Can I stop counting?"

"I suppose so."

"OK," said Charlie.

For perhaps five minutes William lay rigid, not moving a muscle. Above him all

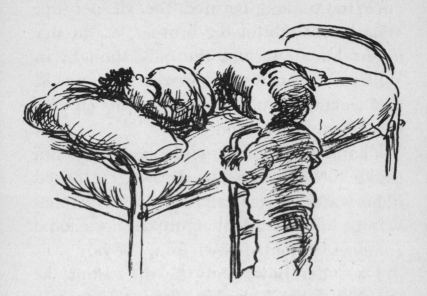

was quiet. Tensely he waited for the next "Will?" It did not come.

Carefully, terribly carefully, William slid from under his duvet and swung his legs over onto the floor. Slowly, silently, he climbed the ladder to the top bunk and peered into it. By the light from the open door he could see the still figure of his brother. Thumb in mouth, Charlie D. Beast was fast asleep.

Cautiously William climbed down again,

picked up Charlie's duvet, scaled the ladder once more, and covered the sleeper up. What a thoughtful big brother, a watcher might have felt, but the only thought in William's head was of Charlie getting cold and waking up and starting up his endless questions all over again.

Thank goodness for wildebeests, William said to himself as he settled down. He looked at his watch. It was half past nine. The room was beautifully silent. Only an occasional small snore floated down from above.

I wonder how many he did count, he thought. I bet I wouldn't have to count as many as he did. It's just because he's small that he had to count for so long. I bet I wouldn't need to count more than a dozen. He pictured in his mind a single wildebeest, starting at the back end with its long tail, the top part like a cow's, the lower part like a horse's with a bushy whisk of hair. He saw its hindquarters sloping up to the high crest of its shoulders, and the thick mane hanging down on either side of its long neck that ended in a huge head, a head too big for the

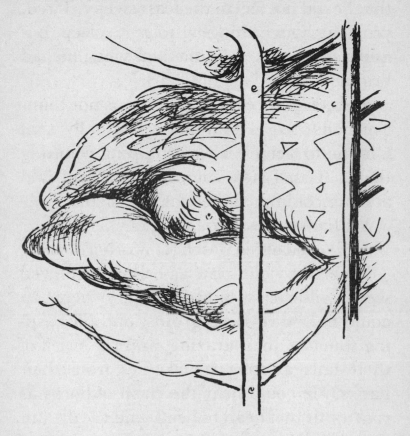

ungainly body, with sharply curving horns
and a great Roman nose and a bearded chin.

Wildebeest number one, thought William. He began to count.

Five hundred wildebeests had marched in

single file past William before he realised that he did not feel in the least sleepy. Tired, yes, longing and longing to go to sleep, but much more wakeful now than when he had begun to count.

Suddenly he realised that it was not counting wildebeests that had eventually sent Charlie to sleep – it was stopping counting them. "Can I stop counting?" he had said and almost immediately he had slept.

William stopped counting.

He looked at his watch. It was ten o'clock.

All around him now as he lay open-eyed were wildebeest noises. Everywhere he could hear their deep grunts, and the rasping sound of their grazing, and the swish of their tails as they struck flies from their flanks. He could hear the clash of horns as rival bulls met head to head, and the distant thunder of hooves as parts of the great herd raced about the African plain. Stopping counting didn't stop them coming, on and on, more and more, in a great black never-ending river of animals.

Wearily, William looked at his watch. It

was eleven o'clock.

Wearily, he dragged himself out of bed and stumbled down the stairs.

In the kitchen, his parents were washing up before going to bed.

"Mum," said William in a moany voice, "I can't go to sleep."

"Isn't Charlie asleep, Will?" asked his mother.

"Yes, ages ago."

"I'll tell you the best thing to do, Will, shall I?" said his father.

"What?"

"Try counting sheep."

Also by

Dick King-Smith

LIGHTNING STRIKES TWICE

Digby has always longed to win a race in the School Sports. But everyone knows he's the slowest runner in the school. What they don't know is that he has Fred, the world's fastest tortoise, to help him beat the record.

When Joanna finds a large black dog lying unconscious in the road and brings him home, everything is turned topsy-turvy. The family soon get used to Yob, but when a burglar breaks in, he gets a nasty surprise!

Two warm and very funny stories by a favourite author.

Tony Bradman

DILLY THE DINOSAUR

Dilly is the naughtiest dinosaur in the whole world.

There was the time he decided he wasn't ever going to wash again. Another day he decorated his bedroom using his sister's best painting set.

And when he *doesn't* get his way, he opens his mouth and lets loose his ultra-special, 150-mile-per-hour super-scream!